Victory!

Brian Brown and Andrew Melrose

CASSELL

For Pearl

Cassell
Wellington House, 125 Strand, London WC2R 0BB

© Brian Brown and Andrew Melrose, 1998

First published in 1998

British Library Cataloguing-in-Publication Data
A catalogue record for this book is available from the British Library.

ISBN 0-304-33678-5

Printed and bound in Great Britain
by the Guernsey Press Co. Ltd, Channel Isles

Titles in
the Storykeepers series

Contents

Chapter 1

Get those Christians!

In the Imperial Palace of Rome, Emperor Nero was in a terrible mood. "… three decades, it's been three decades since we got rid of that … what's his name, that carpenter and STILL those Christians choose to worship him instead of me. Why, he even caused my own centurions to let me down. It was on my birthday too."

"Yes, Caesar," grovelled Snivilus Grovelus, Nero's chief sniveller, "Tch! Tch! Even centurions? Which centurion? Not me, great Caesar, oh noble one…"

"No! Not you, Snivilus. It was Tacticus. On my birthday I said to him, 'You are planning on worshipping me, aren't you, Tacticus?' And do you know what he replied?"

Snivilus had just opened his mouth, when Nero spoke again, "Tacticus said 'I cannot. I cannot!' But why? It is because of those Christians."

Nero arose from the imperial throne and roared through the palace. "Tell Nihilus I want all those Christians DEAD!"

Nihilus had heard Nero shouting, but was keeping his distance for the time being. He had tried to stop Tacticus from escaping but failed, allowing some Christians to escape too. So now, as far as Nero, Nihilus and the Roman army were concerned, Tacticus was a traitor and an outlaw and they would do anything to catch him and the other Christians – anything.

As the full moon flitted in and out of the shadows, Tacticus looked at his new Christian companions. Miriam, a very pretty young woman, smiled shyly at the big centurion, while Ben the baker, a leading storyteller in the Christian underground, steered his baker's cart down another alley. He was leading Tacticus and Miriam to safety. It was a job he had done many times for Christians.

"You know, Tacticus," said Ben, "that Nihilus is evil and he meant what he said. We have escaped for now, but he is out to catch us all, including you. Nero hates Christians even more now that you, one of his centurions, have made a fool of him. He will want us dead and he will make sure Nihilus hunts us down. We are all in even more danger than before."

"I know, Ben," sighed Tacticus.

"I'm afraid your old life as a centurion and mine as the Empress's maid in the Imperial Palace are over," added Miriam.

The big centurion smiled. "I know," he said again, before taking Miriam's hand and adding, "but at least we are together. That way I will be able to repay you for helping to save my life when Nihilus came after me."

Miriam smiled again at the handsome centurion and squeezed his hand back. "We helped each other. That's what we Christians do."

Just then, Zak, Ben's young apprentice baker, slapped Tacticus heartily on the back, "Welcome to the Christian underground, centurion, you're in a real army now."

"Thanks, Zak," laughed the centurion, "I'll remember that."

Tacticus didn't laugh long though, because his thoughts once again turned to his new enemies, Nihilus and Nero. The reason for this was quite simple, of course. Nero, the Emperor of Rome, hated all Christians. So much so, that he had sent many into slavery, or worse: he had had many of them fed to the lions during the Imperial Games. Tacticus knew all this because as a soldier he had seen it with his own eyes. He and Miriam had much to worry about in their new life together.

*

Next morning, in the bakery where Ben and his wife Helena worked and lived, and where Miriam and Tacticus had been taken to hide, the tall soldier stretched stiffly.

"Oh dear, Tacticus," said Helena. "Did you sleep badly, down here in the bakery? Things are a bit tight in here since we took in the children, Justin and little Marcus, Anna and Cyrus, when they lost their parents in the great fire of Rome. I'm afraid we lost the use of our upstairs guest room."

"No need to worry, Helena. I'm just grateful it's not

one of Nero's dingy dungeons I had to sleep in."

"Amen to that," added ten-year-old Anna. "After the great fire and before Ben took me in here, I was hiding in the catacombs. It was like sleeping in a dungeon."

Tacticus ruffled Anna's hair. "And it was down there you saved my life, don't forget." Tacticus went on, "I always seem to be getting my life saved by Christians. First Anna then Miriam, last night."

"But what about you saving all our lives last night," chipped in thirteen-year-old Justin and his four-year-old brother Marcus.

"Yeah!" added Cyrus, the little African juggler, who was just a couple of years younger than Anna. "That Nihilus would have had us all for sure."

Tacticus chuckled at the youngsters' enthusiasm before turning to Helena, "Helena, what's Ben up to?"

"Oh, he and the boys are getting ready to go and bring Miriam's parents over to the bakery. Just in case."

"In case of what?" asked the centurion.

"Oh," hesitated Helena, "...in case Nihilus goes looking for Miriam and then decides to do something nasty because she's not there."

"Then I should help."

"Not this time, Tacticus. It's too risky. The streets will be crawling with soldiers looking for you." replied Ben, who had just returned to gather the boys. "Come on then, Zak and Justin. The wagon's ready."

Chapter 2

Rescued?

Later in the day, as Ben, Zak and Justin sat astride the wagon, which looked as though it was loaded with bags of grain, Justin leaned over and slid back a loose floorboard. "Are you OK in there?" he asked courteously.

"I'll be much better when we can see Miriam again. How much further to the bakery?" came a low voice. It was Samuel, Miriam's father.

"Almost there, Samuel. Just sit tight," replied Ben.

"Sit tight! Did he say sit tight, Laura?" muttered Samuel as he tried to get comfortable in the tight compartment Ben had rigged up in the wagon to help them to escape.

"Oww! Watch those bumps, Ben. Otherwise I'm going to be bruised all over." Samuel grumpily tried to get comfy again. "Huh! One minute you're a first class citizen. The next minute you're travelling economy class in a baker's cart."

"Well, Samuel, that's what we get for raising our daughter as a Christian," replied Laura, proudly, before kissing his latest bruise.

"Ow!" grumbled Samuel again.

Everyone else just laughed.

Suddenly, Zak sat up straight. "Hush, everyone! Justin, close that hatch. That's a soldier's chariot up ahead. We've got company."

Justin pulled the hatch back to hide the passengers again then, shading his eyes against the sun, he studied the oncoming chariot. "Do you recognize him, Ben?"

"Yes. It looks like Capella. One of Nihilus's men."

The chariot, followed by two men on horseback, drew up alongside Ben and the boys. "Halt! Who are you and where are you going?" asked Capella.

"I'm a baker, sir, and we're off to the miller's with this load of grain we have just collected."

Capella peered into the wagon, suspiciously. "Grain, huh? Well, we'll see about that."

Capella drew his sword and stabbed several times at the grain bags. Justin bit his lip when once or twice the sword went perilously close to where Samuel and Laura were concealed.

"Humph!" said Capella, finally, as he gave the wagon one last swipe with his sword. "All right, on your way."

But that last swipe did it. It dislodged the false board.

"Wait a moment. What's this?!" blustered Capella.

"This is good-bye. Hupp!" shouted Zak to the horses, as he steered the cart around and headed off in the opposite direction.

"Oh good, I do love a chase. After them!" screamed Capella to the two horsemen, as he jumped back into his chariot. "Don't let them escape! Nihilus will reward us well."

Chapter 3

The chase

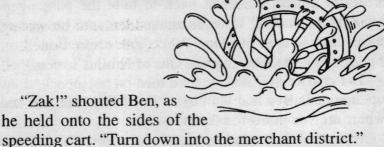

"Zak!" shouted Ben, as he held onto the sides of the speeding cart. "Turn down into the merchant district."

"You mean the place we nearly fried in," replied Zak, recalling the time Nihilus almost burned them out by hurling fireballs from a giant catapult.

"That's the place," replied Ben. "Perhaps we can lose them in the narrow streets."

As the cart whipped down the burnt-out alleyways of the old merchant district, Justin looked over his shoulder, anxiously. "They are gaining on us."

"Here I come!" cheered Capella. He was obviously enjoying himself.

Suddenly, Zak threw Justin the coil of rope which had lain at his side. "Justin, quickly, the beam," he said, pointing at a blackened building.

Justin needed no other advice. He could see the burnt-out building was being held up by one rotten beam. He quickly tied one end of the rope to the back of the cart and then made a loop with the other. Then, after spinning the loop above his head, he lassoed the beam.

"Bull's eye!" shouted Ben, as the cart pulled the beam down and the building began to fall behind them.

"Oh!oh! You have cut off the horsemen but Capella was too quick. He's still on our tail ... and now he's breathing down our necks."

"Zak! Look out!" cried Justin suddenly, to the young driver. But he was too late. While Zak concentrated on the driving, Capella cracked his whip and it wrapped around Zak's arm.

Capella yanked the whip and Zak yanked back, but the centurion was much too strong for the young apprentice baker and he was pulled right out of his cart, straight into Capella's chariot.

"Well now, look who's dropped in," laughed the centurion, as he shoved Zak over the front of his chariot.

"Zak!" shouted Ben, as Justin took the reins of the cart. "Hold on!"

"Don't worry!" replied Zak, as he clung to the tongue of the chariot and struggled to stop himself from being dragged head first under the speeding wheels.

"Hey, baker," shouted Capella to Ben. "Give it up! You can't outrun me."

"That's what you think," mumbled Zak, in reply. He had an idea that just might work.

As Capella drove his horses on, Zak leaned down and pulled the pin out of the joint which connected the chariot to the horses.

"Bye!" Zak shouted as he jumped back into Ben's cart, just in time to see Capella's chariot going in the opposite direction to his horses and then careering out of control, straight into the river Tiber.

"Hurrah!" cheered Ben and Justin together.

"Hey!" moaned a very bruised Samuel from inside the secret compartment. "Can we slow down now? The only thing I have left to bruise is my … ouch! Too late. I'm now bruised all over."

"Not long now," said Justin, reassuringly, as he slowed the cart down to baker speed.

Chapter 4

Tight squeeze

"Mother, Father," said Miriam, hugging her parents.
"Oh, I am so pleased to see you safe and sound."

"Sound!" answered Samuel. "I can hear sound … It's ringing in my ears. Young Justin here may be a good driver but he needs a comfier cart. I ache all over from bouncing around in that thing."

"Never mind your father, Miriam," said Laura. "He always has aches and pains. It's lovely to see you."

"Come into the bakery, everyone," summoned Helena, "soup's ready."

"Mmm! Smell that," said Ben, patting his over-large stomach. "I'm starved and Helena makes the best soup in all Rome."

"Oh, Ben," nudged Anna, as she passed him some freshly baked bread. "You're always starved."

Ben chuckled as the gang sat down to eat.

At the other end of the table, Ben, Miriam and Tacticus were busily looking at a map. "Now," said Ben, "Saleem's boat will be in port next week, right. Near this, uh, carrot?!"

"Sorry, Ben," called Marcus.

Ben smiled and quick as you like popped the carrot into his mouth.

"Once he arrives, we'll sneak you down to the port. Night time will be best. Under the cover of darkness."

"But not undercover in that cart, I hope," chipped in Samuel. "My back still aches."

All of the kids laughed. They were getting used to Samuel's aches and pains.

Ben laughed too, "We'll see," he said. "But meanwhile, until then you'll be safe here."

"Then that must be the friendly neighbour banging on the door," countered Samuel.

The others froze at the sound of the loud knock at the front door as Zak looked to Ben for guidance.

"Quick," whispered Ben to Miriam, Tacticus, Samuel and Laura, "you hide. Justin, you and the others know what to do. Double speed."

As Ben walked slowly to the door, Miriam wriggled into a giant urn, and Samuel and Laura eased into a cupboard. "Yow!" whispered Samuel, "watch my corn."

"I think I need a bigger pantry," panted Tacticus in a hushed voice, as he tried to squeeze himself in.

"I'm afraid it's one-size-fits-all," replied Justin. And with a mighty shove, he and Zak pushed Tacticus into the pantry and slammed the door shut.

"Well it doesn't fit me," came a muffled reply from Tacticus inside the pantry.

"Phew!" said Zak, "I'd hate to try and do that with Stouticus." Stouticus was the fattest centurion in the entire Roman army.

"Or Ben!" giggled Justin. Zak laughed too.

"What are you two laughing at?" asked Helena. "Come, get these aprons on and get baking. Ben's about to open the door."

"Aaargh!" yelled a startled Ben, as he stared up at two gigantic, identical looking brothers.

"Aaargh!" the identical brothers yelled back, equally startled, before stepping in through the door and knocking Ben over.

Zak stiffened and grabbed a large frying pan as the brothers bounded into the bakery. Just then someone spoke.

"Tracus, Bracus, that's no way to greet a customer!"

"Phew!" said Ben, as he picked himself up and dusted himself down. "It's OK, everyone. It's just Antonius the miller, with the new delivery of flour."

"Sorry about Tracus and Bracus, Ben. Just got them and they are not quite house trained. Raised by wolves and all. Quite a bargain though. If only they would stop chewing my sandals. Look." Antonius held up a raggedy sandal, "That's the third pair in a month they've chewed. It's worse than having a dog."

"Yes, I see what you mean." replied Ben, as he dusted himself down.

"Never mind, though. They'll soon have your flour delivered. Come on, you two," commanded Antonius. "Jump to it."

Chapter 5

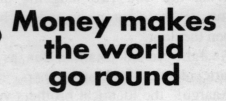

Money makes the world go round

Very soon Tracus and Bracus were unloading the heavy sacks of flour and dropping them near the pantry door.

"Now that's six bags of ..." said Antonius, absent-mindedly, as he began tallying on his pocket abacus, "Christians at ... oh! Oh my! Don't tell me you're hiding Christians in here again, Ben."

Ben looked a little sheepish, "Em, as a matter of fact ..."

"No," said Antonius, covering his ears, "I said don't tell me! Now," he said, returning to his abacus, "Now I have to charge you more."

"But why?" asked Samuel.

"Delivery to Christians. High risk, you know."

"Antonius, we all have to do our part."

"Oh very well. I'll waive the fee ... this time. That will be ninety sesterces, please."

Helena counted out ninety then passed a bag of coins to Antonius.

"Ah well, the sacrifices I make in the service of Jesus. Come along, boys," he called, as Tracus and Bracus dropped the last of the flour by the pantry.

As Antonius, Tracus and Bracus finally left, Zak turned to Ben and said quietly, "I don't trust him, Ben. The way he carried that money out of here, he reminded me of the story of Judas."

"Who's Judas?" asked Marcus, as he joined Ben.

"He's the disciple who turned Jesus over to his enemies, Marcus," replied Zak.

"That's right, Zak," said Ben as he ruffled Marcus's hair. "You see, Marcus, it was just before the great feast of Passover. Sit down and have some more of Helena's delicious pastries, and I will tell you the story.

"For some time," continued Ben, "a group of priests and elders had become angered by Jesus' teachings. They heard that he claimed to be God, which was a crime worthy of death. And they were afraid Jesus would cause riots and then the Romans would punish all of them. So, they decided he had to be stopped, but how? Jesus was far too popular to be arrested publicly.

"Jesus seemed to be unaware of the resentment he was causing, or at least if he knew it did not stop him going about the people and spreading his teachings.

"Finally, after looking to the High Priest, Caiaphas, for leadership, the priests reasoned it would be better that Jesus should die, than to risk punishment of all the people by the Roman army. But they were still not sure how they could do this.

"Then one day, someone told Caiaphas that one of Jesus' twelve disciples was willing to betray Jesus to them. His name was …"

"Judas!" interrupted Zak.

"Quite right, Zak!" said Ben. "Judas Iscariot, to be precise.

"But there was a price. Judas would have to be paid. Caiaphas listened to this information, then reported it back to the priests. They agreed immediately to pay a sum of money.

"So, Caiaphas sent his messenger back to Judas. On hearing that they had agreed to his terms, Judas sent word back to the Council, saying he would alert them when there would not be any crowds around Jesus."

"What a dirty trick!" interrupted Anna.

"Yeah!" agreed Justin. "Then nobody would see Jesus being arrested."

"So what happened, Ben?" asked Cyrus. "Did Jesus get away?"

"Well, not quite. A lot happened after Judas had agreed to alert the Jewish Council."

Anna was most upset. "I can't believe one of Jesus' friends would do that to him."

"Me neither," said the little African juggler. "You don't think anybody would turn us in, do you, Ben?"

"I certainly hope not, Cyrus, but we can't be too careful. Many Romans turned Christians in during the great fire. They were scared, many still are. And people do things for all different reasons."

Chapter 6

Fate comes knocking

"Go on with the story, Ben," shouted Justin. "What happened after Judas agreed to …" Justin didn't get a chance to finish because suddenly everyone jumped.

"Who can that be knocking on the door now?" asked Helena anxiously.

"I don't know," said Ben, "but I reckon it's a friend. Enemies usually come straight in through the front door."

"Ben!" came a shout from the back door. "It's Darius, open up."

Ben opened the door and Darius, an old friend of Justin and Marcus's parents, came rushing in. "Ben, the city is crawling with guards. They are everywhere."

Ben peered out of the window to take a look.

"They are going from door to door," continued Darius, "and they …" Darius paused, "they are looking for Tacticus and Miriam."

Anna let out a huge sigh as she gripped Tacticus by the hand.

Ben turned to Tacticus and Miriam. "OK, you two, we've got to get you to the catacombs right away. You will be able to hide there."

"The catacombs?" gasped Miriam, "Where all those old bones are?"

"Don't worry, Miriam," said Tacticus. "That is where I met Anna. She saved my life down in the catacombs."

Miriam smiled at the handsome former centurion as they gazed into each other's eyes.

Helena, clearing her throat, said, "You'll need food, water and blankets."

"Right, Helena," directed Ben, taking control. "Quickly, you and the boys stay and get the supplies together. Zak can bring them when you're ready. The rest of you, come with me."

*

Meanwhile, elsewhere in the city of Rome, Bracus and Tracus were pushing a millstone round and round, grinding out flour.

"Fifty sesterces, sixty sesterces, seventy sesterces, keep at it, you two. You keep grinding the flour and I'll let you know how much we are earning. Eighty, ninety, one hundred. Oh, I do like counting the sesterces."

"Do you indeed?" asked a gruff voice, suddenly.

"Wh … why, C-Capella," mumbled Antonius.

"Hello, miller."

"Uhm, c…can I get you some flour? I have some very fine corn flour, or perhaps you prefer wheat?"

"What about Christians?"

"Oh, oh!" giggled Antonius, nervously. "I'm fresh out of Christian flour I'm afraid."

"Really?" replied Capella, menacingly. "Well, this morning you were fresh in! I encountered them on the way here. A little fat baker and his boy helpers."

Antonius raised a single eyebrow, warily.

"Help me find them, miller, and there will be a reward for you."

"A reward!" responded Antonius, this time with great enthusiasm. "And what might the reward be, oh excellent one?"

Capella grabbed Antonius by the tunic and leered at him. "Your life!"

"Gulp!" went Antonius, as Capella's grip tightened. "Well now, since you put such a high price on that particular merchandise, I just might have *something*."

Capella had a sly grin on his face. "Oh good!" he said.

Chapter 7

Catacomb capers, revisited

"Cough! cough! By the time Zak gets here with the supplies," shouted Ben, through the dust, "this place will be fit for a king."

"Ouch!" shouted Samuel, as he hit his head on the low roof. "He'll need to be a very short king."

*

Back at the bakery, Helena, Justin, Marcus and Cyrus were packing the wagon, supervised by Zak.

"All right, everyone," Zak commanded. "Let's roll."

"Wait!" added Marcus, as he ran back inside.

Zak put his hands on his hips. "Now what?"

"You forgot Leo and Theo."

"Who?" asked Zak.

"My lions, remember."

Zak did indeed remember Leo and Theo, the real lion cubs who ate his tunic. "You mean those lion cubs who nearly ate me?"

"No, silly, my toy ones." Marcus came out holding two stuffed toys.

Justin shook his head at his little brother. "They don't

need your old lions in the catacombs, Marcus."

"No?" asked Marcus, wide eyed.

"No!" said Zak.

"But Miriam might get scared in those old cat combs. Leo and Theo always look after me when I get scared."

"That's very thoughtful, Marcus," said Helena, ruffling his hair. "Food and clothing are important but sometimes we need more than that. Gather round, everyone. Let me tell you."

Helena sat down, with Marcus on her knee. "You know, Jesus had a friend named Mary who knew this. And although a lot of people didn't like her, she was very special to Jesus. One night Jesus and his disciples were having dinner at a friend's house and Mary came to visit. Well, this made some people angry.

"'Doesn't Jesus know what kind of woman she is?' asked one.

"'This is no place for a woman like that,' grumbled another.

"But Mary pushed her way through, saying, 'Out of my way, I will come in.'

"As Mary pushed her way through to Jesus, someone else said, 'If he really is a prophet, he would know what kind of woman she is.'

"The woman finally reached Jesus and she looked up towards him. She seemed nervous and frail, until Jesus looked at her compassionately. Then she took a flask out from beneath her robe, opened it and poured the ointment over Jesus' head.

"'That expensive perfume should have been sold and

the money given to the poor,' Judas muttered.

"Jesus' disciples were confused. But Jesus smiled at the woman and put his hands on her shoulder. Then he turned to the crowd and spoke:

"'Leave her alone. Why do you want to upset her? It is a fine thing she has done.'

"Then Jesus pointed to the door. 'There are always poor among you. You can help them whenever you want. But I'm not here forever.'

"Touched by these words, the woman left Jesus, moved through the crowd and walked down the street. And Jesus said that what that woman did would be told all over the world."

"Just like we are telling that story now," added Justin.

"That's right," said Helena. "Just like Christians scattered all over the world are doing now."

"Er! Talking about scattered Christians," interrupted Zak, "We will be scattered too if we don't get a move on. I think I hear doors being battered down. The guards are on their way."

"Yes," urged Helena, "You're quite right, Zak. We'd better get these supplies out of here. They might make the soldiers suspicious."

Chapter 8

Ben's last supper?

In the catacomb cave, Miriam and Laura finished sweeping.

"Why don't we all have a seat?" said Ben. "I don't know about the rest of you but I have worked up quite a hunger."

As the others gathered round, sitting on the newly dusted rocks, Ben pulled his satchel towards him. "Bread!" he announced, pulling his hand from the satchel. "I always carry some," he reached into the satchel again, "and a little wine. Bread and wine, it's not a feast but it should be enough to keep us going."

Tacticus nibbled at the bread and sipped a little wine. "I wonder if this is how Jesus felt on the night of his last meal with his friends."

"I hope this won't be our last meal, Tacticus," sighed Samuel, heavily.

"Of course not. But it's my first meal as a wanted man. And Ben, didn't you say Jesus knew he was a wanted man on that night of the Passover?"

"Yes, Tacticus, that's right. But he knew more than that, which gave the disciples quite a surprise. You see, they had all gathered for the Passover meal in the upper room of a man's house, in Jerusalem, when Jesus spoke to the disciples. He said: 'One of you sitting here having supper will hand me over to the leaders.'

"The disciples were astonished. 'Hand him over? What's he talking about?' they muttered among themselves. Then they began to deny it. 'It's not me,' one said. 'Nor me,' said another. One even said, 'I'm not the one, am I?'

"Jesus said nothing.

"One disciple asked, 'Who would do that to you?'

"Judas looked up as Jesus said. 'It is one of you. He is here sharing this very meal with me.'

"Then unnoticed by the other disciples, Judas got up and headed for the door. But before he left, he heard Jesus say, 'It will be a terrible thing for whoever hands me over to be killed. It would be better for him if he had never been born.'"

Samuel, Laura, Miriam and Tacticus ate on in silence, as Ben broke more bread while he talked.

"But you know, that night Jesus did something new. He took some bread, and after he gave thanks he broke the bread into pieces and gave it to the disciples. As he handed the bread to the disciples, Jesus said, 'This is my very self, my body broken for you.'

"As the disciples took the bread and ate it, Jesus poured a cup of wine. Then he took the cup, gave thanks again and gave the wine to the disciples, saying: 'This is my very self, my blood. I will die, then all people will know God loves everyone, everywhere.'

"And the disciples drank from the cup."

Tacticus, Miriam, Samuel and Laura said nothing at that point, as they too passed around the cup of wine which Ben had poured.

*

Back at the bakery, Zak called out to Helena, "Right, that's it. The cart's loaded."

"Be careful, Zak," said Helena anxiously.

"Don't worry, I'll be back soon. I'll stick to the back roads."

"Hurry off then, Zak," said Helena. "There is someone at the front door of the bakery."

"Who?"

"They are asking us to open up in the name of Nero. It's the guards. Hurry, go."

Helena ran back into the bakery then shouted to Justin, Marcus and Cyrus, "OK, boys, business as usual. Justin, you get the ..." Just as Helena was about to say "door" the door crashed in.

"Nihilus and Capella," whispered Justin to the others. "With the two horsemen we outran yesterday."

"Well now," grinned Nihilus, "and you must be the fair Helena. So very pleased to meet you. Your friend, the miller, sends his regards."

"Antonius," whispered Cyrus, "so Zak was right not to trust him."

As Nihilus tried hard to be ever so pleasant, Capella and the other guards had been searching the bakery.

"No sign of the baker or anyone else, sir," said Capella.

"Do a proper search," said Nihilus, as he angrily smashed a pot. "Ransack the place. I want them found."

After much destruction, Capella said again, "Sorry sir, the baker is just not here."

Nihilus smirked and eyed Helena and the boys, "Oh well, no matter. He soon will be."

Chapter 9

Burn
the bakery!

Nihilus pushed his way past the smashed front door of the bakery and strode outside and began shouting. "Listen up, you Christian dogs!" he bellowed.

Zak immediately pulled the cart over to listen.

"If any of you see the miserable, fat little baker they call Ben, you tell him he has until sunset to show his face … or his bakery will burn!"

Zak was aghast. But just as he was about to get moving, he realized Nihilus hadn't finished.

"And it will burn with his wife and children still in it."

*

High in the Imperial Palace, Nero rubbed his hands with joy. "Did you hear that? Did you, Snivilus? Did you hear it? Nihilus will burn that horrible little bakery down if that frightful little baker doesn't return. He's a marvel, a marvel. I should have promoted Nihilus a long time ago."

"Oh yes, Caesar, marvellous, simply marvellous. You were so right to promote Nihilus. He'll do the job of catching all those Christians. No doubt," grovelled Snivilus.

"Catch them? Catch them? I want that fire first. I like fires, you know that."

"And for good reason, Caesar. You are the world's best fire maker, after all."

"Snivilus, I hope you don't mean what I think you mean."

"Uhm, er, n-no, your excellence. Absolutely not. We all know it was the Christians who caused the great fire of Rome."

"Precisely, Snivilus. So never forget it."

"How could I forget, your excellence? They set fire to the whole of Rome. Why, even my own house …"

"Oh shut up, Snivilus. Do you really have to mention your own little hovel when you are here, in the Imperial Palace?"

"Yes, Caesar, I mean no, Caesar, I mean …"

"Snivilus!" shouted Nero.

"Shutting up, Caesar," grovelled the little toad.

*

Zak was very shaken by Nihilus's announcement, but he managed to get to the catacomb cave to tell all. "That's what he said, Ben. If you're not back by sundown, he'll burn the bakery down with Helena and the boys still inside."

Ben rubbed his hands together, anxiously. "We've got to get them out of there."

"How? Nihilus has the place completely surrounded."

"Then I have to give myself up."

"Ben, you can't."

"I have no choice, Miriam."

"Maybe you do," added Anna.

"Anna," sighed Zak. "I'm telling you, there is no way on earth to get near that bakery."

"But we're not on earth anymore, Zak."

"Huh!"

"We're under it," smiled Anna, who looked as though she just might have an idea. Anna tossed a shovel to Tacticus and shouted, "Come on!"

Tacticus and Samuel grabbed the torches and followed Anna out of the cave and into the catacombs. But Zak backed the other way.

"Zak," hissed Ben. "Where are you going?"

Zak frowned, then said "I'm going to make that miller pay. He betrayed you, I know it."

As he ran off, Ben shouted, "Zak, no, come back!" but to no avail. Zak was gone.

Chapter 10

Truth or untruth

Capella was pacing the floor of the bakery. "Look, you little brats. The baker's wife is out in that kitchen worried sick about you," he snarled. "Tell me where big Ben is and I'll let you go back to her."

"No!" Marcus snapped back.

"But why?" wheedled Capella.

"Because you're bad!" said the youngster.

"Marcus, shh!" urged Justin. He did not want the guard getting angry.

"The boy's right, Capella."

The boys turned round to see Nihilus standing in the doorway, again. "You should show some respect. These are children, after all."

"Yeah!" said Cyrus. "Some respect."

"Not only that," continued Nihilus, as he kneeled down and looked straight into Justin's eyes, "they're orphans."

"H-how did you know that?" asked Justin. Nihilus had struck a raw nerve.

"Oh, I know all about you. It's only right you should

feel some loyalty to the man who took you in. But what you don't realize is that man is a traitor to Rome."

Justin was confused. "That's not true."

"Oh yes it is. Not only that, he's a liar. He's not trying to find your parents. It's just a trick to keep you here."

"Why would Ben do that?" fumed Cyrus.

"Why, to keep you all working in his bakery, for free. Does he pay you? Does he?"

"N ... no," stammered Cyrus.

"Well, there you go, then. Now I could really help you."

"He can," ventured Capella. "Nihilus is now one of the most powerful men in all Rome."

"That's right," agreed Nihilus. "I'm Nero's number one!"

"How?" asked Justin. He was very nervous. "How could you help us?"

"I could find your real parents."

Justin and little Marcus gasped. They hadn't seen their real parents since the first night of the great fire. They always tried to hide their feelings but they missed their parents so terribly and often talked of them when everyone else was asleep.

"I could make you a family again," added Nihilus, as he moved closer to Justin. He sensed he had made a connection. "All you have to do is tell me where the baker is."

The huge centurion stood up and Justin looked up at this giant of a man. "Think about it, kids," he said, gruffly. "I'll be outside."

Nihilus and Capella left the bakery through the smashed door and left the stunned boys alone.

*

Meanwhile, just across the street from the bakery, Miriam poked her head over the top of a small drainage grate. "We'll never make it at this rate."

Tacticus puffed, as he and Ben shovelled earth using the two little shovels they had been using to clean the cave. "We have to. Anna is right. A tunnel is the only way."

"I just hope we are in time," puffed Ben.

"Keep digging," said Samuel, ignoring his bleeding thumb, as he clawed at the earth with his bare hands. "We have to be in time."

*

Antonius was sitting at a desk, balancing his ledger, when suddenly the door burst open. "You!" said the startled miller. "Do your Christians need more flour already?"

"Don't try to bluff me, miller," snapped Zak. "I suppose you're surprised I'm not trapped in the bakery, like the rest of them?"

"Trapped? In the bakery...? What are you talking about?"

"Nihilus is going to burn it!"

"Oh!" muttered the miller.

"With Helena and the boys still in there," spat Zak.

Antonius was visibly shaken, "I ... I don't know what

you are talking about. I'm sure I don't ... Tracus! Bracus!"

Zak drew his sword back. "You can lie to me, but you can't lie to my sword."

As Zak was about to bring his sword down, Bracus grabbed him from behind.

"Is there anything wrong, master?" asked Tracus.

"No. This young man is just leaving."

"This way, then," urged Bracus, roughly, as he shoved Zak out of the door.

But Zak wasn't finished, and he called out, "I don't know how you can live with yourself, miller! I know I couldn't!"

Zak's words stung home and Antonius winced. "Tracus, follow him home and report back to me. I want to know what he does next."

*

Zak made his way through the back streets of the city. Tracus trailed him at a discreet distance. Soon enough, Zak slipped around the back of a deserted building and Tracus just managed to get close enough to see him slipping into the catacombs, where Ben and the others were busily digging. Tracus, having seen enough, secretly turned to leave.

*

At the bakery, Nihilus sat at the kitchen table and began sharpening his sword, when the children entered from the back room. "So, the discussions have taken place. That didn't take too long. What have you decided?"

Justin cleared his throat. Since he was the eldest, he was elected spokesman. "Well, sir, we thought about it, and, well, we do want to find our real parents."

"Good, good," smirked Nihilus, triumphantly.

"Yes," added Cyrus, "and we decided the only fair thing to do would be to put your generous offer to a vote."

"Commendable idea. I agree," smiled Nihilus.

"All those in favour," said Cyrus, "of telling this lying man who burnt down half of Rome and is now pretending to be our friend where Ben is say 'aye'."

A hush descended on the bakery. No one said a word.

Then all together the boys said, "NO!"

"Then the no's have it," announced Cyrus, "It's a ... uhm, oh yes, a nanny moose."

"... er ... agreed," added Justin.

Nihilus was seething angry but he did not let it show. "So your vote was unanimous."

Cyrus blushed.

"Fine, as you wish. But," added Nihilus, with a menacing sneer, "let's see if your Baker Ben can save you now."

The big soldier rose angrily and kicked over the table as he grabbed his sword and left the bakery.

"Oh, boys," cried Helena, as she hugged Justin, Marcus and Cyrus, "I'm so proud of you."

"Why?" asked a curious Cyrus. "We only did what anyone else would do."

"Anybody except that miller," volunteered Justin. "I can't believe he squealed on Ben."

"Yeah, he's just like Judas," added Cyrus.

Helena ruffled Cyrus's hair. "But you know, Cyrus, Judas wasn't the only one who let Jesus down."

"Really?"

"That's right. After their last supper together, Jesus and his disciples walked to the Hill of Olives. It was on the road to the village where they were staying. Jesus had been walking in front, when he suddenly turned to his disciples and said, 'You are all going to run away. You will all let me down.'

"Peter said, 'I'll never do such a thing. I won't let you down!'

"All the other disciples nodded in agreement. But Jesus said, 'Peter, before the cock crows twice, before dawn tomorrow, you will have said three times that you do not even know me.'

"Peter was adamant, though. 'I'll die for you first!' he said.

"But," said Helen, with a sigh, "Peter did not realize what he was saying. Jesus and his disciples had come a long way together since those happy days by the lake side in Galilee."

"And so has Ben, and so have you, and so have we," blurted little Marcus.

"Helena," said Justin, quietly, "what are we going to do?"

Helena said nothing. She really did not know.

Chapter 11

A day of reckoning

Early in the evening, Tracus finally returned to Antonius's mill. "Well?" asked Antonius, "What have you to report?"

"The youth …"

"Zak."

"Yes, Zak. He went into the catacombs in the city. It looks like they are trying to dig their way to the bakery."

"Really?" said Antonius. "Show me where. Bracus, you may as well come too."

In the catacombs, a very dirty Ben was near exhaustion. "We should be getting close now," he panted, "just a few more feet and …"

"BAKER!" shouted Nihilus, again, from the front door of the bakery. "I know you're out there."

"Nihilus!" wheezed Ben, to Samuel and Tacticus. "He must be right above us."

"BAKER!" shouted Nihilus again. "This is your last chance to save your family. Or soon … THEY DIE!!"

"Ben," urged Tacticus. "It's my turn to dig. Don't worry, my friend. We'll make it."

Ben smiled lamely. Then suddenly he heard Tacticus's shovel making a loud clang.

Samuel heard it too. "What is it?"

Tacticus pulled the dirt away with his hands, revealing a huge wall of rock. "It's a boulder."

"Oh no!" cried Anna, "and we are so close."

"Quickly," wheezed Ben, "let's get the dirt away and see if we can shift it."

*

As the sun finally dropped behind the Palatine Hill, Capella rubbed his hands with a little glee. "Huh! I knew that coward of a baker wouldn't show."

Nihilus nodded then pointed to the bakery. "Board it up and burn it down."

"Aye aye, sir!" saluted Capella. "OK, men, you heard the order. Board up the bakery and burn it down."

"Oh dear," said Stouticus, who had been drafted in for fire duty. Stouticus was the fattest soldier in the entire Roman army and he had fond memories of the bakery. "They did such lovely light pastries and bread that always tasted so fresh and yummy. Oh dear, I wonder if I might get some before they torch the place."

"Stouticus," yelled Nihilus. "Get more oil. I want all of Rome to see the blaze."

"Oh well," thought Stouticus. "That's that then. I could have done with a snack too. It's just about time for one. Dinner was over about an hour ago…"

As Stouticus waddled off for more oil, the other guards began boarding up the bakery.

Inside the bakery, Helena and the boys huddled together when the banging began.

"Helena," repeated Justin, "what are we going to do?"

"Hush!"

"Helena?"

"Shh! I think I hear something."

"What?"

"Shh!"

Helena and the boys were quiet for a moment when suddenly they could hear a faint clanging sound coming from underneath the bakery floor.

"It's Ben!" shouted Cyrus, "Everybody, dig!"

Helena and the boys grabbed anything they could, cups, pots, spoons and bowls, and began digging.

Outside, Nihilus was surveying the bakery. "You there, fat one, Stouticus, dump that barrel of oil around the sides."

As Stouticus struggled with the barrel, Nihilus took a lighted torch from Capella. "All right, baker, you asked for this!" Nihilus lit the kindling wood and the bakery went up like a roman candle.

"Whoosh!"

Miriam, who was still peeking over the drainage grate, gasped. "He did it, he set it on fire!"

"Wonderful!" screamed Nero, gleefully from his Imperial window. "He did it. He set it alight. Wonderful! Oh, I do love a good fire."

"We're not going to make it, Ben," said Laura.

"She's right, you know," said a strange voice.

Laura jumped back.

Zak drew his sword, "You!"

"You'll never make it with those puny shovels," added Antonius, "Tracus, Bracus!"

Tacticus held Zak back, as Tracus and Bracus stormed into the tunnel with gleaming new pick-axes and began hacking away furiously at the huge boulder.

"Phew! It's hotter than a baker's oven in here," complained Antonius.

Ben was flabbergasted, as Tracus and Bracus kept digging. "Antonius, I … I don't understand."

Antonius gestured to Zak. "Your young friend here was right … I couldn't live with myself if I let that monster, Nihilus, do this to you."

Ben clasped his arm and Antonius blushed. "Besides, you have been a good customer," he said, tongue in cheek. "I'd hate to lose you."

"God bless you, friend," said Ben.

"No, Ben, God forgive me."

*

In the bakery the boys continued digging but it was getting very smoky inside. "Cough! Cough! Hurry," shouted Justin.

Little Marcus hugged Helena tightly. "Justin," he shouted, "Justin, cough, I'm frightened."

"Hurry! Cyrus," shouted Justin again.

Cyrus was sitting in a hole of earth, "I'm hurrying as fast as I ca … a … a … whooaaa!!!" Suddenly, a gigantic hand had emerged from the dirt and pulled Cyrus deep into the hole.

"Where did he go? Come on, Cyrus, this is no time to be messing about."

"Justin," shouted Marcus. "The flames!"

"Cyru … ahhh!" shouted Justin as another hand

grabbed him and pulled him into the hole too.

"Justin? Justin? Where are you … aahhh!" screamed little Marcus, as he too was grabbed.

Justin, Cyrus and Marcus lay in a heap at the feet of Tracus as Helena peered through the hole at them. Then she saw Bracus reach up for her.

"Gently, please," pleaded Helena, "Gently …!"

"Who's Gently?" asked Bracus, as he yanked Helena into his arms. Tracus shrugged, "I don't know. But I'm hot. Let's get out of here."

"Gladly," said Helena, as she straightened her tunic.

"Who's Gladly?" asked Tracus.

Bracus shrugged, "I don't know. But I'm hot too. Let's get out of here."

Tracus and Bracus urged Helena, Justin, Marcus and Cyrus up the tunnel.

"Gently," said Tracus, thoughtfully, as they walked up the tunnel, "maybe that's your Christian name."

"Gladly," nodded Bracus, "maybe that's yours."

"Hmm!" said Tracus, "Gently and Gladly."

"Yes!" said Bracus, "Gladly and Gently."

"I like it, Gladly!"

"Me too, Gently!"

The two great big twins, Gently Tracus and Gladly Bracus slapped each other with joy as they celebrated their new Christian names.

"We're Gently and Gladly!" they shouted. "Or Gladly and Gently! Whichever you prefer."

"What are you two wittering on about?" asked Antonius.

Chapter 12

No looking back

Next morning the air around the burnt-out bakery still smelled thick with smoke. As Nihilus and Capella surveyed the scene a guard approached.

"I don't know what happened, sir. But they are gone. There is not a trace of them. No bones, nothing."

"But that can't be," gasped Capella.

Nihilus cast Capella a wicked glance.

"Search again. Nero wants to see evidence."

The guard walked off and began searching again.

"Stouticus, you fat oaf! You help!" yelled Capella.

"Help!" came a muffled cry.

"Stouticus, are you shirking?"

"Help!" came another muffled cry.

"What's going on over there?" called Capella.

"It's Stouticus, sir, he's disappeared."

"Disappeared?" Capella was getting very angry. "Why that fat, good for nothing … If I find him eating, why, I'll …"

"Help!" came another muffled cry.

"Where's that coming from?" asked Capella.

"Down here! I'm down here."

"Stouticus!" yelled Capella. "Is that you, Stouticus? What are you doing? Where are you?"

"Down the hole."

"What hole?" Suddenly Capella fell down the hole too.

"Ouch!" complained Stouticus, as Capella landed on him. But he didn't want to annoy his superior officer. "I fell, sir, honest. And it's not a hole, it's a tunnel," said the fat centurion.

"A tunnel! A TUNNEL!" fumed Nihilus, as he reached down and grabbed Capella's tunic. "Capella, I don't care if you have to dig up all of Rome! You find that baker. Do you hear me, Capella? Find him! Or this tunnel will be put to better use when we bury you up to your neck, so the crows can peck your eyes. Do you hear me, Capella?"

"Loud and clear," gulped the soldier, as he climbed out.

Chapter 13

Justin's big moment

"Phew!" said Ben, next morning, as he looked around the catacombs. "I think we must have nearly all of the Christians left in Rome down here."

"And look how hard they are all working," added Helena.

About forty Christians were working in the catacombs. Some were filling water jugs, others sewing blankets, some were even making new candles.

"Excellent work, everyone," encouraged Ben. "Another hour and we can break for lunch."

"Already," said Helena, as she pinched his big tummy.

"Well," laughed Ben, "I can't be the only one who is hungry."

"Ben," called out little Marcus. "How much longer do we have to stay down here?"

"Just five more days, Marcus. Then Saleem's boat will take us to our new life in Shemhadar."

The little boy was none the wiser, "What's in Shem ha ha?"

"Not Shem ha ha, Shemhadar."

"Well, what's there?"

"Freedom, Marcus, freedom. You see, it's an oasis that sparkles like a jewel in the desert, where cool clear water from an underground stream ripples into a shimmering pool. And it's surrounded by luscious palm trees. But most importantly, it's a place where the Romans aren't in charge. Travellers from all over the world meet there to trade with each other. From Shemhadar, we can tell them our stories and they will take them back with them, all over the world. Would you like that?"

Marcus nodded and giggled as Ben tickled him, "Now where is that brother of yours?" asked Ben.

"Over by the well," giggled Marcus.

Ben strolled over to the well. "Ah, Justin. I've been looking for you."

Justin lowered a bucket into the well. "Just finishing up, Ben."

"You know, Justin, your fourteenth birthday isn't far off. I think you're ready to take on an important new job."

Justin smiled. "Gosh, Ben, thanks. What is it? A courier? A scout?" Then he whispered behind his hand, "A spy?"

"Something even better than any of them," replied Ben.

Justin looked bemused. "What, then?"

"I'd like you to tell the story at tonight's meeting."

"Huh? Y...you want me to tell the story?"

Ben put his hand on Justin's shoulder. "Why not? You're one of the best students I've ever had. You know our stories backwards and forwards."

Justin was nervous already. "But not well enough to

tell them to everyone. Why can't you tell the story?"

"Well," said Ben, "I could, but there may come a time when I can't. If the stories are to be passed on, then all of us must become storykeepers."

Justin grinned, sheepishly, but didn't reply.

*

Up on the surface, away from the safety of the catacombs, things were getting tense.

"A full week! A full week of digging and still nothing. Capella, you are going to pay for this." Nihilus was at his most menacing.

"Sir," cried a footsoldier, "the Christians caved the tunnels in behind them."

Nihilus sneered. "Then un-cave them. I don't want excuses, I want results." Furiously, Nihilus kicked over the remains of Helena's charred table.

"Ouch!" shouted Capella, as the top hit his arm. But he didn't feel the pain for long because something caught his eye.

As Capella peered down at the wooden table top, Nihilus scowled at him and shouted. "What are you looking at, Capella?"

"It's a map," replied Capella, "Look!"

"Why Capella, so it is," said Nihilus. "Well done. And look, their hideout is clearly marked. Well done, Capella! There will be no escape for those Christians this time." Nihilus laughed a wicked laugh, as the other Roman soldiers looked on in bewilderment.

*

Back in the catacombs, Justin was getting very anxious. Little Marcus whispered to him, "But, Justin, you've told me these stories lots of times."

"But that was different, Marcus," replied Justin. "You're my little brother."

"Hush, everyone, please! Justin?" said Ben, as he gestured Justin to come forward.

Justin stepped forward, then he coughed, then fidgeted, then coughed again.

The crowd grew restless. "What's he doing?" someone asked.

"I don't know," said another. "Is he lost?"

"Perhaps he forgot," said a woman at the back.

"Look!" said her friend, "the boy's shaking."

Justin just stared at them, "I … I …" he began, then he ran.

"Hey! Where's he going?"

"Justin, Justin," shouted Ben, as he got ready to chase after him.

"I'll go, Ben," said Helena, "you stay here,"

"Well," said Ben, with a big smile, "I guess Justin just wasn't ready." Then he smiled again. "Of course, neither were the disciples when Jesus said one of them would betray him."

As Ben began to tell the story, Helena caught up with Justin, by the well. "Justin," she said softly, "It's all right."

Justin shook his head. "But I let Ben down."

Nero's soldiers were looking for Ben

Jesus and his friends sat down

"I'll die for you first!" said Peter

"Board it up! Burn it down!" he said

One of the guards found a map

A garden called Gethsemane

Jesus let Judas kiss him

Ben and Marcus in prison

"Nail him to a cross!"

Meanwhile Ben was in trouble

"That's the end of the story," said Capella

A large elephant broke in

"You should have escaped when you had the chance," said a guard

"Why are you weeping?"

Capella was dying

Saleem's ship sailed away

"Oh, Justin, Ben understands. You're not ready, that's all."

Justin frowned. "I'll never be ready."

"You sound just like Ben when he started out. You know, the first time he told a story, he was shaking so badly I thought we were having an earthquake."

"Really?" smiled Justin.

Helena nodded and winked, then put her arm around Justin's shoulder. "Come on, let's go back and listen."

Back in the main meeting area of the catacomb, Ben was continuing with the story. "...as Jesus and the disciples walked up the Hill of Olives, Jesus turned to Peter and said, 'Before the cock crows twice tomorrow, you will say three times that you do not even know me.' Peter was very concerned and replied, 'I will die before I betray you!' The other disciples were just as firm. 'I'll never let you down. We'll stay with you no matter what,' they said.

"Well, Jesus kept walking up the hill and the disciples followed until they reached a garden called Gethsemane. It was late in the evening, and Jesus asked Peter, James and John to come with him into the garden and said to the others, 'Sit here until I have prayed.'

"As Jesus, Peter, James and John walked deeper into the garden, Peter said, 'What's wrong, master?'

"And Jesus replied, 'I am broken hearted. My soul is full of grief. Stay here and keep watch.'

"Well, Peter, James and John were very concerned as they watched Jesus walk a little beyond them, fall to the ground and begin to pray. 'Abba! Father!' Jesus prayed.

'You can do anything. Don't let me go through this terrible suffering. If it is possible, rescue me. But I will do what you want, not what I want.'

"The garden was still as night, as Jesus got up and walked back to Peter, James and John, but they were asleep.

"'Simon Peter, are you asleep? Couldn't you keep awake for one hour?' Jesus looked disappointed, then said to them, 'Keep awake and keep praying! I know you want to help me but you're just not strong enough.'"

Ben looked up at his friends gathered in the catacombs. "I would have stayed awake," said Zak, in determination. "I would stay awake for ever if need be."

Ben smiled, "Yes, Zak, I am sure you would try. But you know, when Jesus returned, after praying again, Peter, James and John were asleep again."

"Poor Jesus," said Justin, who had settled down beside Marcus and Zak, "he must have felt so alone. Just like Marcus and me until we find our parents."

"Oh but Justin," said Helena, "you're not alone. We are here."

Justin smiled warmly.

"Anyway," said Ben, "getting back to the story. Jesus was still in Gethsemane praying when some Roman guards came into the garden. So he turned to the sleeping disciples and said, 'Are you still sleeping? The time has come. He's here …'

"It was Judas. He approached with the Roman guards. 'Get up!' said Jesus to the disciples Peter, James and John. 'Let's go! The one who betrays me is here!'

"As the guards trampled through the garden, Judas turned to the head officer and said, 'The man I kiss is the one you want. Arrest him and guard him closely when you take him away.'

"Judas approached and kissed Jesus, then the guards swooped and seized him. The disciples rushed to the scene and couldn't understand why Jesus did not try to escape. Then a scuffle broke out and one of the disciples struck a guard with a sword. But Jesus did not want this.

"'Stop!' he shouted. The disciple dropped the sword and joined the others who had run away."

"What cowards!" shouted Zak.

"Shh!" said someone at the back.

"Tell us what happened then, Ben," said another.

"Well," said Ben, "Then Jesus turned to the guards and said, 'Did you have to come armed with swords and clubs to take me like a common criminal? I spoke day after day in the Temple in front of everyone. You didn't arrest me then.'"

"Then what, Ben?" asked Cyrus.

"Then," said Ben sadly, "then they led Jesus away, out of the garden."

There was silence in the catacombs as the story began to sink in. Little Marcus turned to his brother and cuddled him, saying, "Don't worry, Justin. You'll tell the story next time."

Justin just sighed. Because before he could get a chance to reply, Capella suddenly burst in. "Remember," shouted Capella, "Nihilus wants them alive!"

But he was too slow for Zak. "Action stations,

everyone. To the defences!"

Zak had rigged up a series of defences against the possibility that the soldiers might find them. Now was the time to put it to the test. His first manoeuvre extinguished the candles and plunged the catacombs into darkness. This confused the soldiers but not the Christians. They had already rehearsed an escape plan.

"Just grab the tunic of the person in front of you and follow the candle at the front," whispered Helena. "That way, God willing, one little candle will light the way for all of us."

Inside the catacombs, the darkness had caused chaos and by the time the guards lit their own torches Capella saw the shambles. "Arrest the Christians! Not each other, you buffoons."

In the confusion, most of the Christians had managed to escape, but Zak had a plan for the soldiers. "OK!" he said to Ben. "When the last Christian goes through the tunnel, release the boulder."

Ben looked up. A huge boulder was being held by ropes and was ready to be released over the entrance to the tunnel, trapping the soldiers inside the catacomb.

"Now, Ben!" shouted Zak.

As the boulder began to roll, Ben suddenly heard a small shout. "Ben!"

Justin ran back into the catacomb. "Ben, it's Marcus. He's still inside."

As Justin ran back in, Zak and Ben wedged a plank of wood under the boulder, to stop it rolling any further.

"I've got it, Ben," shouted Zak, "you go!"

As Justin pelted rocks at the soldiers to create a distraction, Ben shouted, "Marcus! Jump!"

"Hurry," shouted Zak, "I can't hold this much longer."

"Come on, boys," said Ben to Marcus and Justin. "Time to go!"

Just then, the plank gave a great creak and the boulder began to roll. It knocked Zak into the tunnel and then rolled over the entrance.

"Oh no!" said Ben. "Now we're trapped inside with the soldiers."

"Well," said a voice from behind them. "If it isn't Ben the baker."

"Gulp!" went Ben.

"Nihilus!" said Marcus and Justin together.

Nihilus smiled. "So nice to meet you at last, Ben. Shall we go?"

Chapter 14

Betray?

In Rome, Senator Patronius had a huge party. Everyone was talking about the capture of Ben.

"Imagine," said one partygoer to Patronius, "one of the Christian underground leaders turned out to be a baker. Whatever next?"

Patronius smiled at his guest. "Maybe now the bread in the dungeons will improve."

"Well, they won't need much," said another guest. "Didn't that Jesus feed five thousand people with just a few loaves? We could save on the dungeon food budget."

Everyone around the room laughed.

Meanwhile, a servant girl walked into the room, offering nibbles. "Honeyed larks' tongues, Senator?"

Patronius was about to dismiss the girl, when he recognized her. "Those tongues are unevenly glazed!" he scolded. "Who sent you out with this tray?"

Patronius pulled the servant aside to remonstrate further.

"Phew!" said one of the guests. "Unevenly glazed? I wonder how Patronius would act if something was really wrong? Is he going to beat her?"

Patronius had taken the servant by the arm and taken her into the garden. "Helena," he said at last, when no one could hear, "thank God you're all right. I'm so glad you came."

"I promised Ben I would, if ever he were in trouble. Is there any word of him?" Helena looked very concerned.

But Patronius didn't have good news. "I'm afraid he's in Nero's darkest, most guarded prison. There's no hope of breaking him out, I'm afraid."

"Oh!" said Helena.

"But perhaps I can help from the inside."

Helena sighed, "But how?"

Patronius tried to console her. "Leave it to me. I will do what I can."

"I know," said Helena. "I know."

*

Down at Nero's top security prison, Ben, Justin and Marcus, along with two other Christians, Vasilus and Philo, who had been arrested earlier, were all in "prison pits". These pits were holes in the ground with bars on top, so that the prisoners had to look at the hot sun all day. Ben was in one pit, Justin and Marcus in another and Philo and Vasilus in another.

"Water ... we need water," shouted Vasilus to the passing Capella.

"Then tell me where Tacticus and the other Christians are hiding!" replied Capella.

"We don't betray our friends!" said Ben, defiantly.

Capella dribbled some water into the pits then kicked

over the water barrel. "Well, today was your first day. Tomorrow it will be just as hot. Perhaps thirst will change your minds."

As Capella and the other guards walked away, Vasilus moaned, "Philo, I don't want to die!"

But Philo was getting a little tired of Vasilus's complaining. "Oh, be quiet, Vasilus!"

Ben was a little more comforting, though. "Everyone is scared sometimes, Vasilus. Why even Peter was scared after Jesus was arrested at Gethsemane."

"He was?" said Vasilus. "I mean, not that I am saying I'm scared. But was Peter?"

"Yes," said Ben, "he was scared. He was so frightened that when Jesus was taken to see Caiaphas ..."

"Who's Caiphus?" asked little Marcus.

"Caiaphas," said Ben, "was the High Priest. As the soldiers took Jesus to see him, Peter followed behind. But he was afraid to be seen. And when Caiaphas and the other leaders gathered to question Jesus, Peter stayed in the courtyard with the servants, warming himself by the fire."

"Ben."

"Yes, Philo?"

"What did Caiaphas and the other priests want with Jesus?"

"Well, Caiaphas and the others questioned Jesus about his teachings. Witnesses were brought forward who told lies about Jesus. But these people couldn't even make their stories fit together. Even Caiaphas was concerned. He said to Jesus, 'Why don't you answer? Why don't you defend yourself?' But Jesus didn't reply."

"Reply to what, Ben?" asked Philo. "I'm confused. What did he want to know?"

"Oh, didn't I say? Well, Caiaphas said to Jesus, 'Once and for all, are you the Messiah, the Great Deliverer? Are you God's son?'

"So what did he say?"

Ben sighed, "Jesus said 'I am.'"

"Phew! And then what did Caiaphas say?"

Ben smiled. He had always been fond of Philo. "Well, Caiaphas was so concerned, he tore at his clothes as he said to the other priests, 'We don't need any more witnesses. You have heard the terrible thing he has said. What is your verdict?'"

"Well?" said Vasilus. "What was the verdict?"

"Guilty," said Ben quietly.

"They all voted that Jesus was guilty and should die."

A hush fell over the prison until Ben began to speak again.

"Anyway, Vasilus, I was telling you about Peter."

"Oh yes, Ben," answered Vasilus quietly.

"You see, after Caiaphas and the religious leaders voted that Jesus was to die, there was a bit of a commotion. For a start the soldiers were unkind to Jesus. They spun him around blindfold and made fun of him, saying, 'If you are so smart, man of God, tell us who hit you?'

"Peter was out in the courtyard and heard the commotion. Suddenly, a maid looked over to Peter. She recognized him and said, 'You were with Jesus, that man from Nazareth!'

"Peter pulled his hood over his face, saying, 'I don't know what you are talking about.'"

"Huh!" said Marcus. "You mean he said he didn't know Jesus?"

"Well, yes," said Ben. "The maid shouted again, 'This man is one of those who followed Jesus.'

"Peter heard a cock crowing in the distance, 'No! I'm not,' he said. The cock crew again.

"'Of course you are one of them,' said another man, 'You come from Galilee. We can tell by your voice.'

"And before the cock crew again, Peter said, 'I swear, I don't know this Jesus you are talking about.'"

"He did it. He did it."

"Did what, Justin?" asked Philo.

"Peter! Before the cock crew twice, he denied knowing Jesus three times."

Philo and Vasilus sighed.

"Well," said Justin, "Vasilus, you can do what you like but I'll never let Helena and the others down."

"Me neither, Ben," said little Marcus.

"I know, boys, I know," said Ben, then as he looked through the bars of his cell pit, he thought to himself, "I wonder what Helena is doing now."

*

Zak knew only too well where Helena was. She was down by Rome's docks, outside a very seedy-looking tavern. "Helena," said Zak, "you can't take us in there! The place is full of thieves and smugglers!"

"Who better?" asked Helena. "Who better than a smuggler can smuggle us out of Rome? Come on, Zak! Have a bit of faith. You watch the kids don't get into trouble. I'll be right back."

Zak, Helena and Cyrus looked around at the men in the tavern. "What a motley crew," said Zak. "I wonder what Ben would say?"

Cyrus put his hand on Anna's shoulder. "Don't worry, Anna. My Dad used to hire circus hands at places like this all the time. Just act natural and nobody will bother you."

Just then, a particularly ugly man pointed to Anna and slapped Zak on the shoulder saying, "Hey! How much for the girl? I need a new house slave."

Anna backed away slowly.

"Sorry," said Zak, "she's not for sale."

The man snarled at Zak. "Well, I say she is."

"Actually," said Cyrus, "she's going cheap ..."

"Cyrus!" shouted Anna.

"A real bargain at only two hundred sesterces," continued the little juggler.

As the stranger smiled, Cyrus held out a bandaged hand, then sneezed and said, "Shake!"

The stranger heard the sneeze then took one look at the bandage and screamed, "Urgh! Unclean, unclean!"

Cyrus chuckled, "It's an old trick my father showed me. Works every time."

"Thank goodness for that," said Anna. "I thought you were going to sell me."

"Anna!" said Cyrus, "Aren't we best friends?"

"No," replied Ben, "his courage was amazing, why…" Just as Ben was about to say more, Nihilus came into the stockade and cracked his whip.

"Silence, baker!" Then Nihilus grabbed Capella by the tunic. "As long as he deludes them with these stories about that carpenter, the more they think they'll be saved. But take the baker away and the flock is lost."

"Our faith is stronger than that," said Ben. "Others will pick up the story when I leave off."

Justin sighed sadly. Now he knew what Ben had meant in the catacombs, and he felt bad that he hadn't told the story there.

Nevertheless, Nihilus just mocked Ben. "But your faith is not stronger than Rome, baker. Soon you'll bend to Nero's power. But first you'll bend to mine."

Nihilus laughed a wicked laugh, then as he fondled his whip, the guards came into Ben's cell and began unchaining him.

Chapter 15

A new storyteller, this time?

"Well, that's it," said Vasilus. "They will whip Ben until he tells him where everyone is."

"Ben will never tell," shouted Justin.

"That's what I'm afraid of," replied Vasilus. "Then they will come for us and beat us. Why should we die too?"

Philo was fed up with Vasilus. "We can't turn them in!"

"Philo is right," said Justin. "Ben said we don't betray our friends."

"Well, Ben isn't here," replied Vasilus.

"But if he was here he'd tell us to be brave, just like … like …" Justin was a little shy.

"Like who, kid?"

Justin took a deep breath, "Just like Jesus was before Pilate."

"Huh! What do you know of that story?"

Justin was beginning to panic and Marcus could see it. "Justin, just tell it to me, only louder."

"OK!" whispered Justin. "I … I know that Caiaphas, the High Priest, had made up his mind that Jesus was dangerous and he decided it would be better to execute him, than for everyone to be punished by the Romans." Justin began to relax a little, as Marcus, Philo and Vasilus listened to him tell the story. "But only Pilate, the Roman Governor," he continued, "had the power to order an execution. The religious leaders told Pilate that Jesus called himself a King. Pilate asked Jesus, 'Are you the King of the Jews?' Jesus replied, 'Those are your words.' But the temple leaders brought many charges against Jesus. One by one they stepped forward. One said Jesus was raising rebellion, another said he told people not to pay taxes to the Emperor. One priest said Jesus wanted to start a war with Rome."

"Did he?" asked Vasilus.

"What do you think?" replied Philo.

"No," said Vasilus, "I suppose not."

"No," said Justin. "You see, Jesus said nothing at all. Pilate asked him, 'Why don't you answer these charges?' But Jesus said nothing."

"So that was it, then," said Philo.

"No," replied Justin. "Not yet. You see, at the Feast of Passover, Pilate used to set any one prisoner free the crowd asked for. But at that time, there were some rebels in prison. Their leader was a man called Barabbas. And when various leaders said his name, the crowd began to chant 'Barabbas! Free Barabbas!'

"Pilate said, 'Would you like me to set the King free?' Some must have said yes, but all Pilate could hear was the crowd shouting, 'Barabbas! Give us Barabbas!' Pilate even quietened the crowd and asked, 'What shall I do with the man you call King?' And someone called out, 'Nail him to the cross.' How the crowd roared their approval," said Justin, flatly. "Pilate didn't really know what to do, I don't think. The crowd yelled 'Hang him on a cross.' Pilate asked, 'But what awful things has he done?' But the crowd just yelled, 'Hang him on a cross. Crucify him!' So Pilate released Barabbas and ordered that Jesus be flogged."

"Oh boy!" said Vasilus. "This is some story, son. Then what happened?"

By this time, Justin had lost all of his nervousness and began to tell the rest of the story. "Well, the guards dressed Jesus in a soldier's red cloak, then they made him a crown from a thorn bush and made him put it on his head. Then they mocked him, saying 'Hail, your majesty' and 'Hail, King of the Jews', and then Pilate gave Jesus over to the guards to be executed."

"Now that is not my favourite story," said Philo.

"Mine neither," agreed Vasilus.

"Justin is right, though."

"What's that, Philo?" asked Vasilus.

"Through all of it, Jesus never gave in," replied Philo.

*

Marcus hugged Justin. "Justin. You did it!"

Justin was a little embarrassed but rightly pleased. "I did, didn't I?"

Marcus hugged his big brother again. "Ben is going to be so proud of you."

Late the next afternoon, Zak, disguised as a slave driver, was walking down by the docks with what looked like a bunch of slaves. In fact, they were disguised Christians looking for Sallicus's boat. "This will never work!" he muttered to himself.

As he turned the corner, a guard suddenly shouted to him. "Halt! What's all this?"

Zak handed over some forged papers. "Rowing slaves for Senator Patronius."

"This isn't signed by Centurion Nihilus!"

"Nihilus? Well, fine. You can explain our delay to Nero himself. The Senator's seeing him tonight."

"Pass through," said the guard.

Zak could only give a sigh of relief.

*

Back in Nero's Imperial Palace, Nero had assembled all the senators and a prisoner.

"Snivilus, read the charges," instructed Nero.

"At once, oh mighty one," said Snivilus. Then taking great care, he unfurled a scroll. "Ben the Baker, son of Simon of Galilee, you are accused of being a Christian leader, of inciting anarchy and rebellion, and…"

Suddenly, Nihilus pushed Snivilus aside and grabbed the parchment. "We all know what the charges are. Treason! Treachery! Sabotage!"

In the background, Senator Patronius began to laugh.

"You find this amusing, Senator?" asked Nihilus.

"Yes!"

"Oh? Then might I ask why?" asked Nihilus.

Patronius stepped forward and examined Ben. "Are we to believe this podgy pastry-maker is the daring rebel who has outsmarted Rome's bravest soldiers for so long? I doubt if he can bend down to tie his own sandals!"

This made the other senators explode with laughter. Patronius winked a secret wink at Ben then patted his ample stomach. "A word of advice, Baker. Bake more, taste less."

This made the crowd laugh even more. Even Ben smiled. Nihilus was stunned. "I tell you," ranted the centurion. "This baker is the man!"

Patronius smiled. "My dear Nihilus, you'll make Caesar the laughing stock of palaces from Gaul to Egypt."

Nero was horrified at this thought. "Release the baker at once!"

As the praetorian guards began to unchain Ben, Nihilus shouted, "Wait!" Then he turned to Nero. "Caesar, ask him."

"Nihilus," said Nero, "Are you trying to make a fool of me?"

"No, Caesar, he is. Just ask him if he's a Christian leader!"

Nero raised his eyebrows and sighed, "Oh very well, Nihilus. But I warn you!"

Then Nero turned to Ben. Just as he was about to speak, Patronius interrupted. "Sire, is this really necessary? Why embarrass your eminent court any further?"

Nero waved his hand, "Oh, formalities! Baker," said

Nero, "are you or are you not a Christian leader?"

Everyone looked at Ben as he swallowed hard. "Yes, I am," he said quietly.

Everyone in the crowd was shocked but Nero jumped into the air. "I knew it! I knew it all the time! Despite the preaching of our gullible Senator Patronius. Take the baker away and kill him!"

Nihilus smiled a wicked grin. "With pleasure, Caesar. Move him out!"

Chapter 16

The dock of the bay

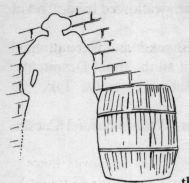

A thick fog rolled in from the river Tiber as Helena, Zak, Marcus and Anna helped the Christians who had escaped from the raid on the catacombs onto Sallicus's boat.

"Let's go!" shouted Sallicus, nervously. "We'll miss the tide!"

"Wait! There's one more," replied Helena, as Patronius approached them in a covered cart. But her face soon turned to sadness.

"I'm afraid I have bad news," he said. "Ben's been sentenced to death. He has two days."

Helena stumbled and Zak and Anna caught her. "Don't worry, Helena, we'll think of something," said the plucky Anna, "we always do!"

As Helena wiped a tear from her eye, Sallicus shouted again. "We must cast off now!"

Helena agreed but then shocked everyone, as Zak and Cyrus gathered by her. She said, "Anna, you go with Tacticus and Miriam. We're staying to help Ben."

"I'm coming too!" said Anna.

"No," replied Helena, gently. "Tacticus and Miriam

are known and wanted. I need you to look after them. We'll meet you in Malta, then leave for Shemhadar together. I promise."

Anna looked at Helena then over at the boat. She suddenly felt small and alone.

"OK," Anna replied.

"Cast off!" shouted Sallicus.

"We'd better be going too," said Patronius. "The task ahead of us is nearly impossible."

Suddenly Zak jumped. "Shh! Someone over there's spying on us." Zak pulled his sword and walked towards the shadows. "You there! Come out or taste this cold sword."

From out of the shadows came a man with a short goatee beard.

"Friend or foe?" asked Zak, when suddenly there was a puff of smoke. It enveloped them both and then when it cleared, Zak was coughing and the man was holding the sword.

"Fortunately for you, friend," said the man, as he turned to little Cyrus. "He is my friend."

Cyrus squinted then said, "Zemo?"

"Cyrus," replied the stranger. "It really is you then?"

Cyrus was very excited. "Everybody, it's Zemo, the magician from my parents' circus!"

Zemo hugged the little juggler. "Imagine their joy when they see you're still alive! They'll be in Rome tomorrow night."

"Wow! Did you hear that, everyone? Anna, Helena? My parents are coming to Rome!"

Anna tried to be happy for him. "That's great, Cyrus."

Helena tried too, but Cyrus could see they were both still sad and he was too.

"Cyrus?" asked Zemo. "What is it? What is wrong?"

"It's Ben," replied the little juggler, "He's been like a father to me since the great fire. And now he's in prison."

Zemo nodded and turned to the sad faces in Patronius's cart. "I tell you this. If the man who's kept Cyrus safe all this time is in danger, then Cyrus's parents, the Great Sabban and Risa, will stop at nothing until he is safe." Then Zemo patted his own heart and said, "And neither will I!"

Everyone gathered round Zemo and Cyrus, as Patronius said, "There's more hope tonight than I had expected."

Even Helena managed a smile. "Come on, everyone," she said. "We have plans to make."

Chapter 17

Capella was there

Down on the river Tiber, a boat sailed gently on the tide, by the light of a pale yellow moon. On the boat, a sailor turned to a beautiful African woman and said, "It's such a fine night. And look over there." He pointed. "It's the lights of Rome, the Imperial city."

"Yes," said Risa, the African woman, "a sight I hoped I would never see again."

"Oh?" said the sailor. "But Rome is the most wonderful city on earth."

Risa sighed, "It was, once."

Just then they were joined by Risa's husband, a tall athletic African man. "You must forgive my wife. Our only son was killed in the Great Fire of Rome."

"I ... I'm sorry," said the sailor, as he moved away to another part of the boat.

"Oh, Sabban," sighed Risa, to her husband.

"Don't worry, my sweet Risa," he replied. "As soon as we meet up with our friends, we'll leave Rome, never to return. Look, the boat is docking already. And we don't have to go ashore."

Risa sighed again. "Are you sure, Sabban?"

"Of course," he replied, "I can leave word for the others. They can catch up with us in Capua."

Just then, they could hear a familiar voice greeting them from the shadows of the foggy dock. "Sabban? Risa?"

Risa smiled and wiped a small tear from her eye. "Good old Zemo. We should have known he would be here to greet us."

"Come then, Risa," said Sabban, "we will go ashore just long enough to say hello."

As Sabban and Risa walked down the gangplank towards Zemo, they noticed a young boy walk out of the shadows and stand beside him. The closer they got the more they thought the boy looked familiar. Just then the boy spoke.

"Mum ... Dad ..."

Risa gasped and held her breath. Then tears of joy flooded from her eyes. "Cyrus! Cyrus!" she screamed. And both Risa and Sabban ran to their son and hugged him.

"Cyrus. Cyrus," Risa kept whispering as she kissed her son. "It's you. It's really you!"

*

Later that night, back at Senator Patronius's villa, the reunion carried on.

Sabban said, "We returned to Rome in hope of finding our old circus friends."

"We never dreamed we'd find our long lost son again,

though," added Risa, as she cuddled Cyrus again.

Cyrus cuddled his mother. "I missed you both so much." Then he suddenly went a little quiet. "I..." his bottom lip trembled a little.

"What is it, son?" said Sabban.

Cyrus smiled weakly. "I just wish Ben could meet you."

"And so he will!" said Sabban. "I'll not let the man who took care of my son die in some dungeon. Especially not one belonging to that tyrant Nero who caused the fire which separated us in the first place."

"Cyrus is lucky to have such fine parents," added Helena, "but you mustn't get involved."

"Helena is right," said Patronius, "it's too dangerous."

Risa smiled. "We appreciate your concern, but we aren't leaving until Ben is free."

"There you go, everyone," said Zemo the magician. "I told you they'd want to help."

But Zak wasn't convinced. "Wanting to help and actually helping are two different things." Then he produced a map of the prison Ben was being held in. "What do a couple of ex-circus clowns know about breaking into the Imperial Stockade?"

Sabban appeared at Zak's shoulder and said, "We know enough to know it won't be easy. But fortunately we have friends in high places."

*

At that moment, Ben was in need of friends. In the prison, Nihilus and Capella were inspecting the prisoners: Justin and Marcus, Philo and Vasilus, and Ben. "Continue to starve them," sneered Nihilus, "except the baker. See that he gets plenty of food. After all, we can't disappoint the lions."

As Nihilus walked out, Capella approached the prisoners. "Just because the baker must die, it doesn't mean you'll have to."

No one replied.

Capella tried again. "Just give me the names of your Christian leaders and you can go free."

Ben smiled. "Perhaps they know something you don't, Capella."

"Like what?" mocked Capella.

"That some things are worse than death," replied Ben.

"Well, baker, that's where you are wrong. Nothing is worse than death; a lesson you Christians should have learned when we executed your Jesus."

Justin stood up. "Huh! What do you know about Jesus?"

Capella snapped at Justin, "I know he died like a common criminal. You see, boy, I was there!"

Everyone in the stockade went quiet, as Capella relayed the story of the events he witnessed.

"Your Jesus had been sentenced to death and was made to walk through the streets of Jerusalem, carrying the cross he would be crucified on. Some of the crowd cried and pitied Jesus, but others jeered and cheered when the guards whipped Jesus to keep going. Just outside the gates of the city, Jesus stumbled and just as the guard was about to whip him again, a Roman centurion took pity and instructed an African called Simon to help Jesus carry the cross up the hill."

"What hill was it?" asked Philo.

"Skull Hill," answered Justin.

"That's right, youngster. In Jerusalem, executions were held at a place called Golgotha or Skull Hill. Jesus wasn't alone that day. Two other prisoners, rebel leaders, were to be crucified as well.

"Jesus was offered wine mixed with myrrh, a spice to deaden the pain. But he refused and he was nailed to the cross. Then they hung a sign on the cross which said 'King of the Jews'."

In the prison, Capella paused for a breath but no one said anything. Then he continued. "As the cross was raised, alongside the other two men, some people gambled for Jesus' clothes. Others mocked him. I heard one man say, 'So, this is the one who would pull down the temple! If you're so powerful, why don't you get down from that cross?' The crowd laughed. A woman said, 'If it's true you saved others, why not save yourself?' Even the religious leaders mocked him. They said, 'Let the so-called Messiah get down from that cross, then we'd believe him.' And so on it went. Jesus hung there for hours, as the crowd taunted and teased him. And then it was all over." Capella paused again and turned to go.

"But why don't you tell the rest of the story, Capella?" asked Ben.

"What rest? He died!"

"Yes. But it was no ordinary death, was it?" Ben

picked up the story where Capella had left off. "Jesus looked down on the people mocking him and spoke. He said, 'Forgive them, father, they don't know what they are doing.' One of the rebels on the other crosses said, 'If you are the Messiah, why don't you save yourself and us?'

"His friend replied, 'Quiet, we're guilty and deserve to die. But this man has done nothing wrong.' Then he turned to Jesus and said, 'Remember me when you are king.' And Jesus said, 'You'll be with me in heaven today.'

"When Mary, Jesus' mother, approached the cross and stood with the disciple called John, Jesus said, 'Mother, take my friend John as your son. And John, take my mother as your mother.'"

Ben sighed a little, before continuing, "Then a little later, the wind began to blow and the sky turned dark and Jesus said, 'My God, why have you left me alone?'

"A man in the crowd said 'He's calling Elijah,' and this started the crowd mocking him again. They did not understand.

"Then Jesus said he was thirsty and a kindly centurion put a wine-soaked sponge on the end of his spear and offered it to Jesus, who drank from the sponge. Then he spoke again. As he said, 'Father, I put my whole life into your hands,' thunder rolled and lightning flashed across the hill and then Jesus said, 'It is finished.'"

Capella grunted, "So there was a storm that day, what of it? The point is, baker, Jesus died and that's the end of the story."

"No, Capella," replied Ben, as he sat down once more. "It's just the beginning."

"Believe what you like, Christian," said Capella, as he moved toward the exit. "Jesus of Nazareth is dead and unless you tell Nihilus what he wants to know, you will be too. All of you."

As Capella walked out of the prison he slammed the door behind him. Ben, Justin, Marcus, Philo and Vasilus said nothing as they pondered their fates in silence.

Chapter 18

Roll up, roll up for the circus

Next morning, while some street performers entertained a group of onlookers outside the stockade a massive elephant balanced a tower of acrobats high on his back. "See," said Sabban to Zak, "I told you we had friends in high places."

Zak turned his nose up at Sabban's little joke but Cyrus re-assured him. "Don't worry, Zak," said the little juggler, "my father's circus friends are just what our rescue plan needs."

Just then the elephant wobbled and the acrobats wobbled too. "If they live that long," said Zak.

Meanwhile, back in the stockade, Capella came to check on breakfast. "Eat up, baker," he shouted, "or Nihilus will punish us both."

Ben walked over to the bars of his cell. "If you let me finish the story you started last night I'll eat every bite."

"That story was finished, baker. Or are you trying to convince me your Jesus didn't really die that day?"

"Oh, he died," replied Ben, "but that doesn't mean the story is finished. You see, a man named Joseph, from the village of Arimathea, went to see the Roman governor and because Joseph was an important member of the Council, he was admitted. The governor, Pontius Pilate, was very suspicious of the council. He asked Joseph what he wanted. Joseph replied that he had come to ask for permission to bury Jesus. Well, at first Pilate didn't trust Joseph when he said Jesus had been crucified that morning. But after it was confirmed he agreed to release Jesus' body so he could be buried.

"It was almost sunset when Joseph got back to Golgotha and when he arrived he was greeted by the disciples and other mourners. They wrapped Jesus' body in linen sheets, which Joseph had bought specially in the city, and then they carried him to a nearby garden, where a tomb had been prepared. Once Jesus was laid to rest in the tomb, the men rolled a large stone over the entrance."

"There!" said Capella, "You said it yourself…"

Ben looked puzzled.

"Jesus was buried. Just like any other man."

"Yes, Capella," said Ben. "But there is more. You see…"

"Wait!" shouted Capella. "What's that noise?"

Capella peered through the window of the prison. "There are jugglers and acrobats climbing all over the roofs. What are they doing?"

Ben looked too. "Perhaps they are advertising their circus."

"Well, Nihilus isn't going to like this," replied Capella.

Just then, Nihilus appeared. "Well, don't just stand

there, Capella, those acrobats may be trying to rescue the Christians."

Justin whispered to little Marcus, "I bet Cyrus has something to do with this."

"Yeah!" whispered Marcus. "Good old Cyrus. I knew he wouldn't let us down."

Capella laughed, "It'll take more than a few circus performers to break into this prison." But he spoke too soon. "Wha … It can't be?"

"It is," said Zak, who was sitting on an elephant which had just broken through the prison wall. "We knocked, but no one answered."

Capella drew his sword. "Welcome! I hope you planned to stay awhile."

Capella charged towards Zak, but the elephant was having none of it and swatted him like a fly.

As Capella lay knocked out cold, Helena searched for Ben and the boys. "Where is everybody?"

"Down here," replied little Marcus through the bars of his prison pit.

Anna looked down. "Don't worry, Marcus, we'll get you out."

"How?" asked Justin.

"Watch!" said Anna as she whistled over to the huge elephant.

The elephant ambled over and stuck his tusks between the bars and pulled. They came away as easy as icing from a cake.

Ben laughed. "I wish we'd had this fellow working for us all along."

"Get that elephant!" shouted Nihilus.

But even Stouticus looked bemused. "How?" he asked as the elephant scooped Ben, Justin and Marcus out of their prison pits.

"Run for the cart," shouted Ben to the others. "I'll be right with you."

As they ran, Helena shouted, "Risa, Sabban, we must split up now. We'll meet you at Saleem's ship."

"All right," replied Risa. "Good luck!"

"Okay, kids," said Helena, "let's get the show on the road."

"Wait," said Marcus, "where's Ben?"

Helena frowned. "Oh, no!"

Chapter 19

The choice

Zak and Helena watched as Ben leaned over to pick Capella up. He was still dazed after being struck by the elephant. Meanwhile, at the other end of the stockade, they could all hear Nihilus shouting, "Capella, I warn you! If the baker escapes it will cost you your life."

"Ben, hurry!" shouted Helena.

But as Capella finally came to his senses, Zak and Helena sensed it was already too late.

"Baker!" said Capella, "do you know what you are doing?"

Ben gave him his sword and said, "Making sure you get to hear the rest of the story, that's what I'm doing."

"Why you crazy, misguided old ..."

Ben looked over Capella's shoulder, then interrupted him, "Please don't kill me, Capella."

"It's Nihilus," said Zak. "He's heading straight for Ben. Come on Helena, we'd better get moving."

"That man," said Helena. "What is he doing?"

"I guess he's made his choice for a good reason," replied Zak, "whatever that is."

"Capella," said Nihilus. "Where are all the prisoners?"

Capella was still dazed as he looked around. "They escaped, sir. All but the baker."

"I would have made it too, if it weren't for Capella," added Ben.

"It's a lucky thing for him you didn't," snarled Nihilus. Then as he grabbed the front of Ben's toga, Nihilus added, "You have interfered with my plans for the last time, baker. Capella."

"Yes, Nihilus?"

"Take the baker to the Amphitheatre. The lions have waited long enough."

Helena and Zak had heard enough and they sneaked off to join the others. "Oh Ben!" muttered Helena. "Why are you always the martyr? Why, you're worse than a naughty child sometimes."

*

While Ben was being led away, two sets of plans were being made.

Justin, Anna and Zak were sitting in a huddle. "Zak," said Justin, "Are you sure we can break Ben out of the Amphitheatre before the lions get him?"

"It'll be just like the last time we saved Cyrus and the others from Giganticus."

"I hope so, Zak," added Anna, "and then I hope we never have to rescue anyone ever again."

Meanwhile, in Nero's Imperial Palace, another conversation was taking place.

"You don't say, Nihilus? Could we, could we really?"

"Imperial Caesar, Nero, I see no reason why not," replied Nihilus.

"Yes, Nihilus," replied Nero, "Why not? Why not indeed? Make all the necessary arrangements."

*

As the wagon carrying Ben travelled across the city, Capella said to Ben, "You should have escaped when you had the chance."

"But then you never would have heard the end of the story," replied Ben.

"How can you sacrifice your life to tell me a story?" Capella shook his head in disbelief.

Ben just smiled. "Maybe you'll understand when you hear how it ends."

Capella just shook his head again.

"Thinking back to that day, Capella, when you saw Jesus on the cross, you may remember a group of women."

"Yes," said Capella, "I do."

"It was Mary from Magdala, Mary the mother of James and Salome. They were there with John the day Jesus died."

"Yes," said Capella, "I remember them. There were also some guards having a conversation at the bottom of Jesus' cross. One of them said, 'Maybe now the Jews can find themselves a real king.' But I remember his colleague said, 'This man was a real king. Surely he was the Son of God.'"

Ben smiled at Capella. Even after all this time he had

remembered. "Those women," continued Ben, "watched as Joseph and the others carried Jesus' body to the tomb they had prepared. By the time they reached the garden it was almost sunset. Shabbat, the Jewish day of rest, was about to begin so they rolled a large stone over the tomb and left.

"The next morning after Shabbat, the women returned to the garden, with sweet smelling oils to put on Jesus' body. But when they arrived at the tomb they were surprised to find the large stone had been rolled away.

"The women went inside the tomb and there was a bright light shining, and a young man spoke to them. He said, 'You are looking for Jesus of Nazareth, the one who died on the cross, but you won't find Him here. He has risen.' The women were frightened and bewildered as the young man spoke again. 'Go tell His disciples He will be in Galilee before you and you will see Him there, just as He said you would.' As the women moved towards the exit," continued Ben, "the man spoke again, saying, 'And don't forget to tell Peter.'"

"What did they do?" interrupted Capella.

"Well, although they were afraid to tell anyone what they had seen, after all, who would believe such a story, they decided to tell the disciples everything. They told the disciples that the man said 'He has risen'.

"Of course, the disciples weren't sure, so Peter and John went to the tomb and found it was true. Jesus wasn't there.

"As the disciples left the garden, only Mary of Magdala remained alone. Then she was joined by a man who asked her, 'Why are you weeping? What are you looking for?' Mary thought he was a gardener.

"Embarrassed by her tears, Mary did not look up. 'Please, if you've carried Him somewhere else, please tell me. I want to go and look for Him. I want to…'

"But the man said, 'Mary, go tell my disciples that I am going to my father. To your father. To my God and your God.' Mary ran to tell Peter and John that she had seen the master."

"Seen the master? So you believe that story, baker?"

"Well, Capella, would I be here if I didn't? The question is, do you?"

Ben and Capella looked at each other, but before Capella could answer the wagon came to an abrupt halt.

"It's Nihilus," said Capella to Ben. "I wonder what he wants."

"Capella," shouted Nihilus, "there has been a change of plans. Nero's orders. The baker is to be taken to the outskirts of Rome and crucified. Fitting, don't you think? Nero is really looking forward to it."

"But what about the Amphitheatre and the lions?" replied Capella.

"Hah!" laughed Nihilus. "Merely a decoy. I knew the baker's friends would surely attempt another rescue. Only this time they walked right into my trap."

"Oh no," said Ben as he looked over as saw Helena and the gang in the other cart.

Nihilus sneered, "Now, baker, all we have to do is wait for Nero and we'll have a party."

Chapter 20

Nero is cross

In no time at all, Nero and Snivilus arrived at the scene on Nero's Imperial chariot.

"Nihilus," shouted Nero, "this had better be worth it. This country air plays havoc with m...mmm...ah choo!"

"Bless you, Caesar," said Ben.

"Pah!" replied Nero. "Come, Nihilus. Let's get on with it."

"Yes, Caesar," said Nihilus, as he carried a hefty mallet and three long spikes towards Ben. But suddenly he stopped in front of Capella. "Why don't you do the honours, Capella? Consider it your reward for foiling the baker's escape."

Before Capella could respond, Nero thrust the mallet and spikes into Capella's hand.

"A...ah choo! Oh do get on with it," shouted Nero, "I think I'm allergic to country air."

As Ben lay on the wooden cross, Capella prepared to strike the first nail into his hand. "I know you don't have a choice, Capella. It's all right. I'm going to be with my Lord."

Capella raised the mallet over his head, then paused. "Yes, but not today." As he swung the mallet down he whacked Nero's chariot and it tipped Nero head over heels into a gully.

"Help!" shouted Nero.

As Snivilus and the other soldiers rushed to help Nero, Nihilus lunged at Capella. "Traitorous dog! You've just signed your death warrant!"

"Death is no longer my enemy, Nihilus," answered Capella, as he drew his sword, "You are."

The two men lunged at each other with their swords. They fought strong and hard and furiously. Meanwhile Ben ran to the other wagon and freed Helena and the gang. "Justin, you drive and don't forget Capella on the way out of here."

"Yes, sir!" answered Justin.

As Justin steered the cart towards Capella, the gang noticed Nihilus had disarmed him and was preparing to strike.

"Quick, Justin," screamed Anna.

But it was too late. "Consider this your dishonourable discharge," shouted Nihilus, as he raised his sword.

As the wounded Capella stumbled forward, Zak reached over and dragged him onto the moving cart.

"Huh! I'm not finished," snarled Nihilus, as he too jumped on to the back of the cart. "Room for one more?"

"Look out!" shouted Zak.

This was the opportunity little Marcus had waited a long time for. As Nihilus pulled himself into the cart, Marcus whacked him over the head with the mallet.

"That's for losing my parents in the fire," he shouted, as Nihilus fell backwards out of the cart and the gang made their escape.

"Phew," said Ben to Capella. "That was some rescue, eh. Eh, Capella?" Ben went quiet. "Capella?"

"Oh no!" said Helena, "He's wounded."

Capella smiled. "At least I got to hear … to hear the rest of the story."

"But there are many more to tell," said Ben, softly, as he held the big soldier.

"And I expect you to keep telling them …" Capella sighed, "… all of you."

Ben mopped Capella's forehead. "You saved us, Capella."

"No!" replied the soldier, softly. "You saved me, Ben."

While Justin drove the wagon to escape, Capella smiled for the last time and then closed his eyes.

*

As evening drew in, Nero was back in his chariot but he was furious. "This is all your fault, Nihilus. You let them escape. You and your ploys and traps. You couldn't trap a legless cat!"

"Pah!" replied Nihilus. "I will have those Christians in chains by sunrise."

"No! You have failed me for the last time. Guards, take him."

Nihilus was stunned. "What is the meaning of this? Seized by my own men?"

Nero raged, "My men. They are my men. I came for a

crucifixion and I'm going to get one."

That was enough for Nihilus. With his great strength he pushed the guards off and grabbed a sword. "The next man who touches me dies."

"How dare you!" fumed Nero.

As Nihilus backed away slowly, Nero ranted after him, "I won't forget this, Nihilus. Mark my words, your days are numbered. Do you hear me, numbered!"

"Yes," shouted Snivilus, as he tried to please Nero, "and numbered days are not good days."

But Nihilus merely responded, "So are yours, Nero. So are yours."

"After him, Snivilus!" shouted Nero.

"M…me? After N…Nihilus?"

"Unless you want numbered days too, numbskull."

Snivilus swallowed hard.

*

Meanwhile down at the docks, Ben and the gang were finally saying goodbye to Rome.

"Safe journey, my friends," said Patronius. "God be with you."

"And with you, Senator," said Helena, as she kissed his cheek.

"Thank you for taking care of Capella," added Ben. "He'd be honoured to know he's been buried in your family vault."

"After all he did for you, Ben, he is family."

Ben and Patronius embraced.

"All aboard," shouted Saleem.

On board the ship, Cyrus sidled up to Ben. "Ben."

"Yes, Cyrus."

"These are my parents." Risa and Sabban smiled.

"At last! I don't know how to repay you for all your help."

"It is we who should repay you, Ben," said Risa. "We owe you the debt," and at that, the beautiful Risa kissed Ben on the cheek.

"Well, my, my," said the red-faced baker, as he blushed. Then he looked over at the docks. "Take a good look, everyone. We won't be coming back."

Anna linked her arm in Ben's. "I can't believe we are finally on our way to Shemhadar."

"Me neither," added little Marcus. Then a second or two later, he added, "Are we there yet?"

Everyone laughed and Ben tousled little Marcus's hair.

Soon Saleem's ship reached the sea and sailed off into the sunset. One of the circus minstrels began to sing:

Oh it's hard to remember the darkness now,
after the fire had burned all our dreams,
and the sky was ablaze, for days and days;
and round every corner
lay strangers and dangers,
until He crossed the sea,
of Galilee,
and said, come walk with me.

As Ben and the gang listened to the minstrel's lilting song, on land, the cloaked figure of Nihilus stood watching the ship pulling away. He listened to the gang join in the song, "… He walked the sea, of Galilee, and said come walk with me …" until he could hear it no more and the ship was no more than a speck on the horizon, then it was no more …

Epilogue

Back on the ship, as Justin, Cyrus and Anna gazed across the open ocean, the little juggler turned to Justin and Anna, saying, "Now that my family's together again, we're going to tour the whole world with our circus."

"That'll be nice," replied Justin. "I don't think Marcus and I will ever see our parents again."

"I know I won't see mine," sighed Anna.

Cyrus looked at his two friends, "Me and my big mouth."

But Anna just smiled at him. She didn't want to spoil Cyrus's happiness, after all.

"Hey!" shouted little Marcus, from the back of the boat. "That funny light is following us. Is it a boat?"

Justin put his arm around his little brother's shoulder, "Oh Marcus, I told you it's just the moon reflecting on the water."

"I don't think so," replied Marcus. "I know what the moon looks like."

Just then, Marcus turned round. "What's Ben doing over there?"

"All right, children," shouted Ben. "We're ready."

"Ready for what, Ben?" asked Anna.

It was Saleem, the boat captain, who replied, "For the wedding."

Anna hugged both Miriam and Tacticus. "I'm so happy for you. I just wish I could give you a gift."

"Actually, you can," replied Miriam.

Anna was confused. "How?"

"Anna," replied Tacticus, "Ben has told us about your parents ..."

"How you lost them in the great fire of Rome," added Miriam.

Anna turned away sadly. "Ben doesn't think they are alive, does he? I know they aren't."

"Well," said Miriam softly, "the gift we really want is for you to be our daughter."

Anna had tears of joy in her eyes. "You do?"

Anna, Tacticus and Miriam all hugged each other in joy, as the ship came in to land.

Marcus turned to Justin, "God's helping everyone to find parents, except us," he said, sadly.

"Come," said Helena, "Give me a hug. God hasn't forgotten you, boys. Just, sometimes it's hard to see what He's doing."

Justin sighed, "I'll say."

As the gang began the walk up the beach and up

towards the higher ground, a familiar figure sitting on a horse called down to them, "What a wedding that was. How touching, Tacticus."

"Nihilus!" screamed Marcus, "I knew there was a boat behind us. He must have been in it."

"Well now, it's Ben the baker and all his little friends," grinned Nihilus. "Seems like you should have listened to the little one. And look who we have here, too. My old centurion friend Tacticus. I see you have a wedding ring on now. How touching. Well, we will soon remove that from you."

Zak drew his sword and charged at Nihilus. But Nihilus just laughed and drew his own sword. "I've sharpened blades on better men than you!"

"Yes, but not quicker," replied Zak as he ducked under Nihilus's sword.

"Wait!" shouted Tacticus, as he drew his own sword. "It's me he wants."

"Well done, Tacticus," taunted Nihilus. "You may have become one of these Christian dogs but at least you're prepared to fight like a Roman. Now prepare to die like one."

"Tacticus, be careful!" shouted Ben, as the two Roman centurions clanged swords.

Suddenly, Tacticus caught Nihilus off guard and knocked him over, sending his sword flying.

But as the two men struggled Ben suddenly shouted, "Oh no! They're rolling over the cliff."

As they rolled, Tacticus managed to get both hands on to an overhanging rock and Nihilus held on to Tacticus.

But Tacticus lost his grip and one hand slipped.

"Looks like you're going to kill me after all, Tacticus," sneered Nihilus, "But at least I'm taking you with me!"

"No!" shouted Ben as he and Zak reached out and began to pull Tacticus to safety.

Nihilus clung on to Tacticus for dear life. As the two men were being pulled up Nihilus spotted a sword on the ground. But as he tried to grab it he slipped back and, with one hand on the sword, he grabbed Tacticus's toga and began to slip back.

"My toga's ripping, Nihilus," said Tacticus. "Here, take my hand."

"No!" roared the evil centurion, "I want your life."

"He's fallen!" said Ben, as Nihilus fell down the cliff for one last time. "Come on, Tacticus. There was nothing you could do. Come on, everybody, let's go, our journey is still far from over."

"Ben," said Marcus, "I'm thirsty."

"Yes," replied Helena, "We all are. But we need to save water until we get to the Shemhadar oasis."

"I think I see it. Just over there," he replied.

"Oh, it's probably just a mirage, Marcus," replied Justin.

"Humph!" replied the little boy. "You said that about Nihilus's ship. But look, now I see Mom and Dad waving."

Justin squinted in the sun, "Marcus, don't start this again. I'm telling you the only thing out there is sand … er … and Mom and Dad!"

"Justin! Marcus!" came the shouts from across the sand.

"Mom! Dad!" Marcus and Justin called back, together, running towards their parents.

"I knew we'd see you again. I knew it!" added Marcus.

"What a wonderful, happy ending to our journey," said Ben to Helena, joyously. "And yet it is only the beginning. As we carry these stories of Jesus and the stories he told, from here to the end of the earth, each of us can be a Storykeeper."

"Even me, Ben?" said Marcus as he hugged his mother.

"Even you, little one," replied Ben. "And as we all pass these stories on, may others come to find the love of Jesus, just as we have. Until one day, there are as many Storykeepers as there are stars in the sky."

– The end –